Sadie the Ballerina

by Joan Betty Stuchner

illustrated by Bruno St-Aubin

North Winds Press

An Imprint of Scholastic Canada Ltd.

The illustrations in this book were painted
in watercolour, on watercolour paper.
The type is set in 16 point Bookman Old Style.

Library and Archives Canada Cataloguing in Publication
Stuchner, Joan Betty
Sadie the ballerina / Joan Stuchner ; Bruno St-Aubin, illustrator.

ISBN 0-439-96109-2

I. St-Aubin, Bruno II. Title.

PS8587.T825S18 2006   jC813'.54   C2006-901981-9

6 5 4 3 2 1   Printed in Singapore   06 07 08 09

Thanks to Rick Welch.
This book is for Tom and Dov and for
all my stage-struck young friends,
especially Naomi Vogt and
Yamit Shem-Tov. Break a leg!
— J.B.S.

Claude and Zoé,
my two favourite ballerinas.
— B.S-A.

Sadie wanted to be a ballerina. She pictured her name in lights on a theatre marquee: *Sadie Levine Dancing Tonight!*

"I'm a natural," she said.
She waved her arms.
She pointed her toes.
She tilted her head.
She tripped on the rug and fell
on her bed.

But she didn't give up.
"Practise makes perfect," she said.

She twirled and tripped again.

4

Sadie watched ballet on television.
She imitated the dancers. She waved her
arms. She pointed her toes. She tilted
her head. She tripped over the cat.

"Merwow!"

"Sorry, Pavlova," said Sadie.
"I guess I need to practise more."

Sadie practised in the kitchen.

"Mom," she said, "may I go to ballet school?"

Mom said, "Oh, Sadie, wouldn't it be more fun to go to clown school?"

Sadie frowned. "But I don't want to be a clown. I want to be a ballerina."

"We'll see," said Mom.

"We'll see" were Sadie's least favourite words.

One day Sadie saw a poster at the bus stop. The big letters said *The National Ballet Presents The Nutcracker.* Below the letters was a picture of a ballerina.

"That's the Sugar Plum Fairy," said Mom.

Sadie posed on her toes.

She tipped over.

"I wish we could see the Sugar Plum Fairy," said Sadie as their bus arrived.

Mom waved her magic shopping bag. "Abracadabra, your wish shall be granted."

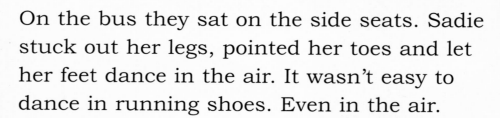

On the bus they sat on the side seats. Sadie stuck out her legs, pointed her toes and let her feet dance in the air. It wasn't easy to dance in running shoes. Even in the air.

People stared. Sadie didn't care.

12

"It's our stop," said Mom.

Sadie stood up, smiled at
the passengers and curtsied.

13

When they got off the bus Sadie ran ahead.
She leapt and twirled. She waved her
arms. She tilted her head. She bumped
into Mr. Chow who lived next door.

"Oops, sorry, Mr. Chow. I was practising.
I'm going to be a ballerina."

Mr. Chow smiled. "It was my fault, Sadie.
I didn't look where I was going."

Dad was home. Sadie couldn't
wait to tell him the news.

"Dad, we're going to the ballet.
We're going to see the
Sugar Plum Fairy."

"Great," said Dad. "I'll dust
off my tux and white necktie."

The evening of the ballet Mom wore a black silk dress. Dad's tux and necktie looked a bit tight. Sadie wore a purple velvet dress with matching silk slippers.

The theatre lobby glittered with chandeliers and rhinestones. It smelled of perfume. "*Whoosh*," said a dress as it swept by, trailing a feather boa. Sadie reached out to stroke the feathers. They disappeared into the crowd.

Sadie's family had front-row seats. The musicians in the orchestra pit began to tune their instruments. Sadie stretched out her legs. She pointed her toes and danced in the air. Silk slippers were better for dancing than runners.

Sadie looked at the stage. She wondered
if the Sugar Plum Fairy was hiding
behind the curtain.

Suddenly the music began. The lights
went down, the curtain went up and
Sadie gasped. Everything was so twinkly!

"Where's the fairy?" asked Sadie.

"*Shh,*" said Mom.

"*Shh,*" said Dad.

"*Shh,*" said the people behind them.

Finally, the Sugar Plum Fairy entered. She wore a pink tutu and matching satin slippers. "Almost like mine!" said Sadie.

"*Shshsh!*" said everyone.

The fairy sparkled and spun.
She tippytoed and flew right into
the arms of the Nutcracker Prince.

It was just too much for Sadie.

Mom was the first to notice. Sadie's seat was empty. "Where's Sadie?" she whispered to Dad.

"I don't know," Dad whispered back.

They looked right. They looked left. They looked down. They looked up. They gasped. Sadie was onstage.

She was running toward the
Sugar Plum Fairy. The Sugar
Plum Fairy looked surprised.

Mom slid down in her seat.
Dad slid down in his seat.
"Oh, Sadie," they whispered.

23

The Sugar Plum Fairy didn't miss a beat.
She stepped forward, arms outstretched,
picked up Sadie and spun her in the air.
Sadie was flying.

"What's your name?" asked the fairy.

"Sadie," said Sadie.

"I'm the Sugar Plum Fairy," said the Sugar
Plum Fairy. Then she winked and handed
Sadie to the Nutcracker.

The audience applauded.

The Nutcracker Prince lifted
Sadie into the air. Sadie gracefully
waved her arms and pointed her
toes and tilted her head.

Then the Nutcracker handed her down to the harpist. The harpist handed her to the first violin. The first violin handed her to the conductor. The conductor handed her to Mom.

Mom plopped her in her seat.

"Stay put, Sadie," she said. This time Sadie stayed put.

The Sugar Plum Fairy and the
Nutcracker finished their dance.
The Nutcracker bowed. The Sugar
Plum Fairy curtsied.

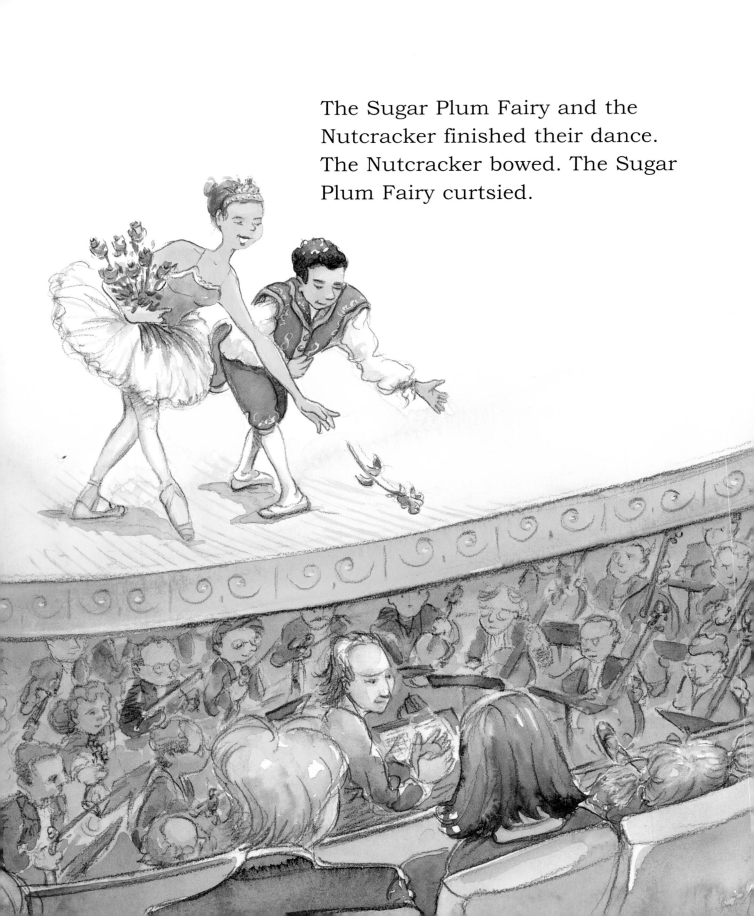

At the curtain call someone handed
a bouquet of roses to the Sugar Plum Fairy.
She plucked out a rose and tossed it into
Sadie's lap. Sadie blushed.

Back in the lobby one of the ushers handed Mom a note. She read it out loud. "Sadie's a natural, but she needs a little practice. I highly recommend ballet school! Love from the Sugar Plum Fairy."

Sadie looked up at her mom. "May I? Please?"

Mom waved her magic evening purse.
"Abracadabra, your wish is granted."

Sadie waved her arms. She pointed her toes.
She tilted her head. She didn't trip.

People stared but Sadie didn't care.

She was going to be a ballerina.